D1251579

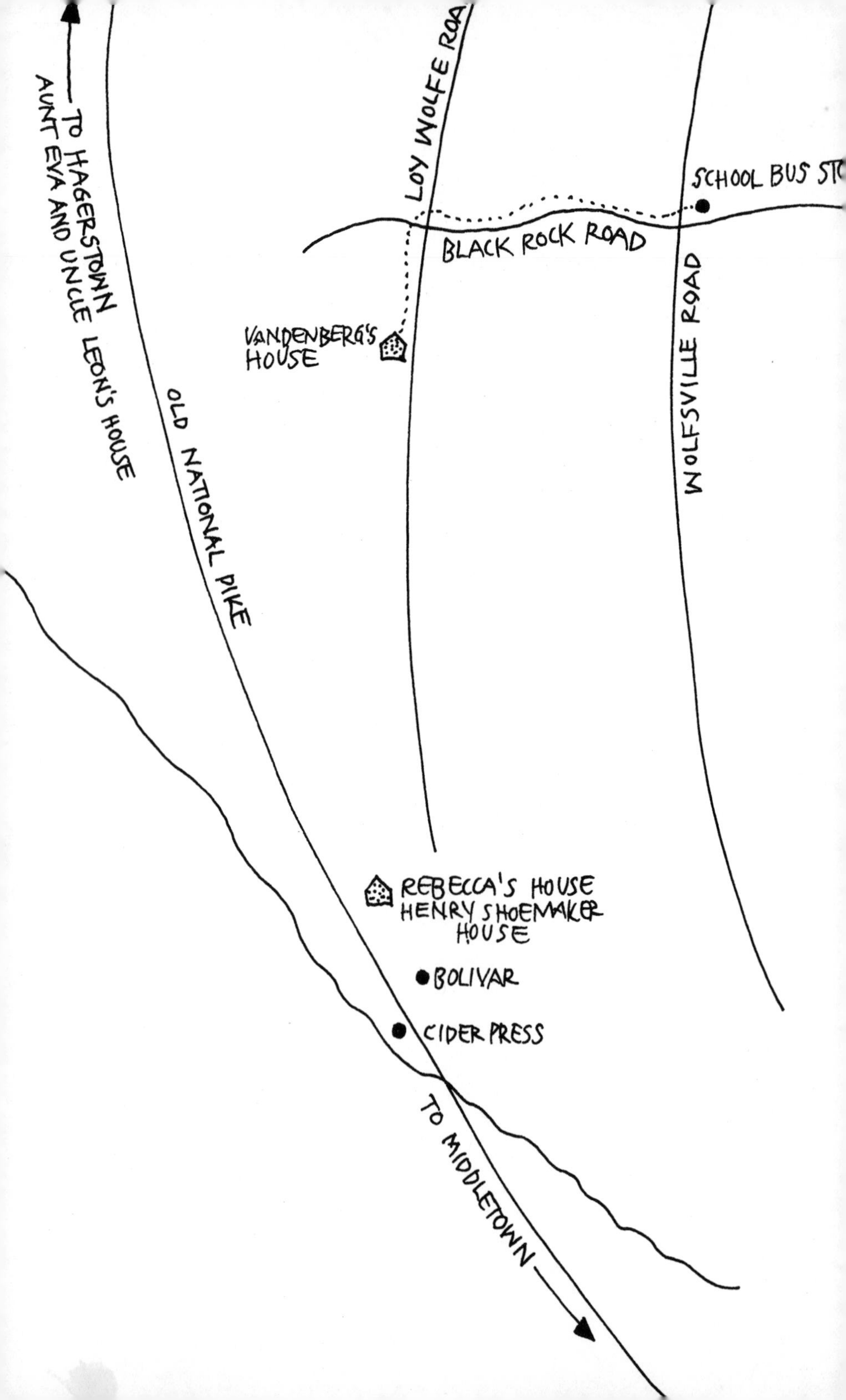
TO HAGERSTOWN
AUNT EVA AND UNCLE LEON'S HOUSE
LOY WOLFE ROAD
SCHOOL BUS STO
BLACK ROCK ROAD
WOLFSVILLE ROAD
VANDENBERG'S HOUSE
OLD NATIONAL PIKE
REBECCA'S HOUSE
HENRY SHOEMAKER HOUSE
BOLIVAR
CIDER PRESS
TO MIDDLETOWN

REBECCA
A Maryland Farm Girl

By Diane Leatherman
Illustrated by Raya Bodnarchuk

Crossing Kansas
Cabin John, Maryland

This book is based on people and incidents from
Rebecca's life. However, some events and
characters are products
of my imagination, so the story must be
considered a work of fiction.

Published by
Crossing Kansas
Box 315
Cabin John, Maryland 20818

Cataloging-in-Publication Data
Leatherman, Diane
Rebecca, A Maryland Farm Girl;
Illustrated by Raya Bodnarchuk
p.cm.

ISBN 0-9665-861-1-5

[1. Historical Fiction 2. Fictional Biography   3. Middle Grade Novel]

Library of Congress Catalog Card Number:2002090822

First Edition
Printed in the United States

CHAPTER ONE
THE ACCIDENT

It was a cloudy, cool September day in 1926 when Poppa brought the wagon around and Momma climbed up beside him. Reminding the children to do what their older sister said, the two parents drove off down the road. They had a load of apples to be made into apple butter and cider, and they were headed to a cider press which was along a creek beside the road on which they traveled.

Poppa smiled at Momma and said, "It's really nice to have some time to just ride along."

Momma smiled back, but she was a little preoccupied with how they were going to come up with money for rent. It was the time of year when the earth gave bountiful gifts, so food was not so much of a problem.

"Whoa," Poppa said, and he pulled on the reins as the wagon went off the road and down the hill toward the creek at an angle. When the horse stopped, Poppa pulled back on the brake and hopped down. Momma climbed down and they worked side by side to unload the apples.

The cider press was under a roof where bees kept company with the men stirring the kettles used to cook the apples. After the apples were cooked and softened to make sauce, after cider and spices were added, it became thick, lumpy brown apple butter which was put into ceramic crocks.

Some of the other apples were pressed and the juice became cider, which was put into barrels. When their crocks and barrel were filled, they were loaded into the wagon. Poppa climbed up on the wagon-seat and clucked to the horse to get going while Momma walked along behind.

The horse strained a bit going up the hill, but Poppa still called out to Momma, "Why don't you get up on the wagon?"

When they were almost to the top of the hill, Momma decided to do just that and, because the wagon was moving so slowly, she just stepped up into the wagon bed. Up front, the horse had just reached the road and, as they began to pull out onto a level place, the wagon sped up. When the wagon itself reached the road, it got going fast enough to skid and one iron-rimmed wheel slipped off the pavement.

On the other side of the road from the creek, there were layers of rock sticking out from the hillside, almost like shelf mushrooms on the side of a tree. The wagon swung forward and sideways, until it lurched off the road and the barrel slid backwards. Momma tried to cling to the back of the wagon, but the heavy, toppling barrel hit her and slammed her body hard against the sharp layers of rock along the side of the road.

"Edna," Poppa called with alarm, feeling the sudden shift. He pulled up the reins and almost fell off the side of the wagon. He stumbled to the back, but it was too late. Momma lay slumped under the barrel which had completely fallen off the wagon. Poppa cradled her in his arms until help came along the pike.

CHAPTER TWO
REBECCA'S SIXTH BIRTHDAY

It had been the spring before when Rebecca pestered her mother yet again, "Momma, are you gonna make me a birthday cake?"

Rebecca hoped Momma would make her favorite, a chocolate cake.

"Git up to bed right now, Rebecca. I've already told you."

Rebecca and her brother, Bobby, washed their faces and hands with a damp cloth and slowly headed out of the kitchen, the scene of everything interesting.

As Rebecca fell asleep that night, visions of chocolate cake floated in her head.

The next day dawned sunny. Rebecca and Bobby rushed downstairs to find a yellow cake, Momma's favorite. Still, it was a cake, today was her birthday, and she was six whole years old. Rebecca was happy.

She and Bobby burst out of the house and raced down to the chicken house to feed the chickens. They only had a few chores of their own because they were still little. "But I'm getting bigger!" thought Rebecca to herself. Getting bigger seemed like a good thing, even with chores.

Their big sister, Geneva, who was considered grown up at sixteen years, and Momma and Poppa had to work most all of the time, but Rebecca and Bobby felt theirs was a good life.

"I love the chickens, Bobby," Rebecca announced to her brother as she scattered the grain. Rebecca knew it was no news to him.

Bobby grinned because, although two years younger than Rebecca, he had tagged along enough to know that his sister talked to the chickens, named and cared about each of them and that they returned the compliment by coming up to her every time they saw her.

After they fed the chickens, they returned to the house to have breakfast themselves. Momma made them each a big stack of pancakes and they ate with gusto.

"I want you two to git me some wood now."

They made several trips to the woodpile because neither could carry more than one big or three small pieces of wood, and that wouldn't have been enough to last any time at all. They did what Momma asked. If they didn't, she might have taken a switch to them and, anyway, it wasn't too much to do.

And then they could play. Rebecca and Bobby had the whole outdoors as their playground, just as long as they could hear if Momma called. They could go to the stream branch and watch the water critters in the shallows. When it was warmer, they could wade in the stream. They could climb the apple tree. They could put down a feed sack to protect their bottoms from splinters and slide down the cellar door.

"Let's make a mud pie in the cat's dish and put six sticks in for birthday candles," Rebecca suggested. Once in a picture they had seen a birthday cake with candles, although they didn't have any on their own cakes. A row of small stones around the outside of the mudpie made a nice decoration.

"Don't you two git muddy," Momma took the clothespin out of her mouth and called to them as she hung clothes on the line.

Their ears perked up when they heard the horse clopping and the wagon wheels coming. "It's Aunt Mae and Aunt Esta and Grandma!" Rebecca jumped up and clapped her hands.

Grandma and the aunties lived up the hill in a nice new house. When she was very small, Rebecca had lived up there with them. Momma had a spell and couldn't take care of her. Rebecca was so small that they carried her around on a pillow and fed her Mellon's Food so she would grow. Grandma knew how to take care of babies because she had fourteen of her own. They told Rebecca that she had go-backs and she was two before she walked. The doctor said it was rickets. After Bobby was born, Momma came out of her spell and Rebecca moved back down the hill.

Grandma was almost as important to Rebecca as Momma. The aunties had told her the story, "Aunt Nellie had to powder her hair white when Grandma went to town because you cried, and we tried to fool you into thinking Aunt Nellie was Grandma."

"Look what we made for you," Aunt Mae called to Rebecca, as they climbed down from the wagon. "Stand still and let me see if it'll fit."

The aunties had made her a new dress! The material came from a feed sack and had little flowers on it. Rebecca couldn't remember the last time she had had a new dress.

"Now we're going to keep it for nice," said Momma. "It should fit you a good, long time."

CHAPTER THREE
GLORIOUS SUMMER

Rebecca and Bobby played hard in the summer sun, but still it was not always easy to get to sleep because there was light outside the window at bedtime. Sometimes they whispered as they fell asleep. Actually, Rebecca whispered and Bobby listened.

Sometimes it was a beautiful story: "And then the fairies came out from under the flowers after all of the people went to bed and danced by the light of the moon..."

Occasionally it was a spooky story: "In our cellar there's a big, black snake and he's waiting for you and me to come down so that he can..."

The stories never ended because the storyteller fell asleep, but that was all right because her audience was already asleep.

For the Fourth of July, there was a Sunday School picnic in the campgrounds, a beautiful glade with big, old trees that Rebecca believed had spirits. Rebecca could feel them as soon as she walked into the glade. The leafy branches cast cool shade on the people eating and relaxing below. Rebecca placed her hands on a trunk and let it tell her stories, stories that couldn't be put into words.

The long tables, made by laying planks over sawhorses, groaned with the weight of Maryland fried chicken, watermelon, potato salad and all kinds of cakes and pies. Momma made a chocolate cake this time, so Rebecca hurried through a big plate full of dinner to get to dessert.

Rebecca and Bobby saw other children that they hadn't seen since last year's picnic. Bobby usually hung back by Momma, but Rebecca always ran to play Blind Man's Bluff, or Red Rover, or Hide 'n Seek with the other children. She played so hard that she fell asleep in the wagon going home and, when no one could wake her, Poppa carried her into the house and up to bed.

As summer passed and everything ripened in the kitchen garden, Momma sent Rebecca and Bobby out to carefully pick and bring in the first tomatoes, then later the beans. Rebecca watched carefully to see if there were going to be any pumpkins for jack-o'-lanterns in the fall.

Rebecca and Bobby picked apples up off the ground; Momma and Geneva cut out the bad spots, canned apples and made applesauce. This was such a rich time of year. There were so many good things to eat, but it was busy, very busy for grownups. Rebecca and Bobby learned to disappear some of the time so that no one would give them another job to do. It seemed that the kitchen was always astir and many times it felt too hot from the stove, where Momma was canning.

Geneva tried to help their mother. She caught the youngsters on Saturday night and brought them in for a scrubbing in a tub in the kitchen after it was filled from the hot water reservoir behind the stove.

"Ouch, you hurt my knee!" said Rebecca, whose knees were always skinned. Sometimes she also had blisters on her hands from swinging on the low branches of the apple tree.

"The hot water's good for your sores," Geneva answered firmly.

CHAPTER FOUR
A SAD FALL

The fall morning when Momma and Poppa were taking barrels of apples to the cider press for apple butter, Rebecca and Bobby stayed home with Geneva because they would just get in the way.

"You two be good now," Momma had said as Poppa hitched the horse to the wagon. He used old Scout to pull the plow most days, although the horse really belonged to Grandma. Momma swung up on her side and after Rebecca and Bobby watched them ride off, they consulted with each other on what to play today.

"There's hollyhocks, ya wanna make hollyhock dolls?" Rebecca asked. One flower would make a petticoat, the other a bonnet. When the hollyhocks were dog-eared after a little play, they turned to corn husks. Corn husks without the grain could become people, whole families of them.

They built houses out of sticks and small stones and "cooked" servings of mud on large leaves. They ran and rolled and climbed trees and hay bales.

There was never nothing to do, but today seemed to drag on for an unusually long time.

The heat of an Indian summer made them feel sleepy. Although Geneva did not make them come in for a nap, they both fell asleep in the shade on the porch.

Still, no Poppa and Momma came home. Geneva looked worried as she dished up cold leftovers for supper.

"When's Momma and Poppa coming?" Bobby and Rebecca asked their sister as they slowly brought the food up toward their mouths.

"Don't you two bother about it. They're coming soon." Geneva answered them, without sounding very convincing.

As the evening wore on, all three of them trudged up the hill, hoping that the rest of the family knew something that they didn't know, but they didn't.

Geneva washed the two children and put them to bed with their questions unanswered.

In the morning when they woke and came downstairs, there were several adults in the house, something that Rebecca couldn't remember happening since butchering time last year. She looked around for Momma, but only saw Poppa sitting in a chair with his head in his hands.

When she entered the kitchen she heard one of the aunts saying, "The wagon swung 'round..." before she closed her mouth on seeing Rebecca and Bobby.

"Would you two like some eggs?" a female voice asked.

"Where's Momma?" Rebecca asked, when she didn't see her at the stove.

The adults looked nervously toward each other, as if each was waiting for the others to speak. Rebecca felt a funny feeling in her tummy. She looked at the two aunts and the neighbor lady and stood her ground. She couldn't say anything more.

Aunt Mae looked gently at the children and said, "Your momma had to go to the hospital. She got hurt yesterday."

"Is Poppa hurt, too? Is that why he's holding his head?" Rebecca was trying to make sense of something that she didn't want to make sense. She wanted to make it go away.

"No, your Poppa's not hurt. But don't bother him now. Can I fix you two some breakfast?"

Rebecca looked at Bobby to see if he looked hungry. Her tummy felt like it couldn't eat until Momma came home.

"When will Momma come home?" Rebecca was sure she asked for them both.

"Not today," was the answer.

Bobby's tummy must have felt like Rebecca's because he followed her out the door and down to the chicken house. Rebecca needed to see her friends and they needed their breakfast. Nothing was wrong with the chickens' appetites.

When she held the gate and looked back at Bobby, there were little tears making paths down his cheeks, leaving dirty streaks. Rebecca put her arms around her brother and tried to comfort him.

"It's gonna' be fine. Momma will get well and come home," she said, although she really felt unsure herself.

They scattered the grain together and Rebecca clucked soothingly to the chickens, then they went to sit under a tree.

Rebecca picked one of the tall, fox-tail tipped weeds and put it in her mouth. She had seen her Poppa do this. It seemed to help him think.

"Maybe Momma fell out of the wagon and that's why she had to go to the hospital."

Bobby choked back a little sob and muttered, not too clearly, "I want Momma."

"I know, me too."

Several days passed. Geneva came back from Grandma's house where she had gone for a while. Her face looked a little puffy and her little sister and brother searched it for traces of information. Grandma came down and cooked for them.

When she could bring herself to speak, Rebecca kept up the questioning. "When's Momma coming home?"

Although he didn't ask, Rebecca knew that Bobby also waited for an answer that was more than the "I don't know" that they seemed to get several times a day from Geneva or Grandma or the neighbor ladies.

They didn't see Poppa much.

Finally, one day the answer was, "Your mother will be home tomorrow."

Rebecca and Bobby woke earlier than usual the next morning and washed their faces and hands, without being asked. They ate breakfast for the first time with some appetite. After they fed the chickens and gathered some wood, they went to sit on the steps and wait for Momma to come home.

Rebecca was drawing little circles in the dust with a stick when they heard an automobile. Autos were pretty unusual, so both children perked up at the sound.

The big, black car came down the hill toward them. Rebecca was all set to see it pass when she realized that it was stopping.

"Geneva, a car's coming...it's stopping!" Rebecca called to her sister, who came out wiping her hands on Momma's apron.

Two men got out of the front and walked to the back. They opened two doors that went all across the back. They reached in together and started to pull something out. It was a very long wooden box.

"What's that?" Rebecca asked her sister, whom she noticed had tears in her eyes.

Geneva answered, "It's Momma."

Rebecca felt as if she had been struck by lightning.

CHAPTER FIVE
MOMMA'S GONE

Grandma said they could have Momma's funeral up the hill in the new house. Poppa said, "This house was good enough for her while she was alive and we'll have the funeral right here."

And so the next day, Rebecca found herself wriggling with a strange excitement while Aunt Velma tried to button her good dress on her. Yesterday, when they had placed the long box in the corner between the windows, they opened the lid and Poppa lifted Rebecca up to see Momma.

One of the grownups said, "She only looks like herself around the forehead." That was all right with Rebecca as she thought to herself that this couldn't be Momma. She was not accepting this new arrangement without Momma.

The house filled with people. Rebecca and Bobby were set on chairs at the foot of their mother's coffin. The preacher's voice went on and on. Rebecca looked out of the long window, which went from the floor almost to the ceiling, and watched clouds move across a blue sky. Everyone bowed their head for a prayer and someone sang a sad song. They closed the lid and Poppa put a spray of lilies, Momma's favorite flower, on the top.

They all filed out of the house and climbed in wagons and autos. It wasn't too far to the cemetery where Aunt Velma firmly took Rebecca and Bobby's hands. They walked across the grass to the spot where there was a hole in the ground. Rebecca couldn't remember anything else that happened that day.

Later, she and Bobby only spoke to each other a little of everything that was happening, but they sensed between their two small bodies a sad understanding of the emptiness that each of them felt. They each knew the other was important to them, but there was no Momma, only a hole.

Geneva did a pretty good job of cooking, cleaning, scrubbing and ironing. She had learned to do all of this in years of working beside Momma. So the household ran pretty much as it always had, except there was one less person and Poppa said very little to them or anyone. No one made jack-o'-lanterns from the round orange pumpkins in the garden but Grandma did make pumpkin pie.

Bobby never said, "'Becca, when's Momma comin' home?" but they both thought it and allowed for the possibility in a fuzzy back part of their brain.

They played, some days almost as hard as the old days, and Geneva scolded them as she gave them Saturday night baths. "You two git so dirty!"

They went up to Grandma's house for some Sunday dinners with roast goose. Rebecca and Bobby listened for the grownups to say something about Momma, something that would allow them to hold on to their hopes that somehow she would be restored, be by the stove in the morning when they woke up. But no matter how hard they listened, nothing was said.

Time passed, slowly at first, and then slightly more normally, until Geneva and Poppa began to talk about Rebecca going to school. Rebecca wasn't even sure when she turned seven, but she was glad that she would finally be able to go to school.

"I want to go too," Bobby said wistfully to Rebecca.

Rebecca tried to imagine school in her head. Geneva had never talked much about her schooling and had quit before Rebecca was aware, so there was no one to ask, not that grownups were much good at answering children's questions.

Rebecca knew there would be other children there. That was a plus. She would walk with Anna, who lived up the road and was eight.

CHAPTER SIX
SCHOOL

Rebecca woke up excited, but Bobby looked wistful.

Geneva plied her with more and more breakfast. "Stop squirming and eat more than that. You'll git hungry before lunch."

When Anna arrived at the door, Geneva handed Rebecca a lunch pail and Bobby waved at her from the front porch where he stood, until she disappeared up over the hill.

It seemed to Rebecca that Anna was very worldly and Rebecca attempted to get some answers about this new adventure before it actually began. "How far is school?" she asked Anna.

"Quarter mile," answered Anna as shortly as possible. She was only bringing this little girl along with her because her mother said she had to "be a good neighbor."

"What happens at school?" Rebecca asked because she needed more knowledge to ask more questions.

Anna was not in a mood to supply many answers but, in her necessary neighborly role, she told Rebecca, "Teacher'll get mad if you talk when you aren't s'posed to and if you don't do your work right. Recess is good. You can play."

Worried, Rebecca asked, "What if I can't do my work; what kinda work?"

"Readin', writin', spellin', cipherin', s'all."

They had entered the school yard by then. The two-story brick building looked huge to Rebecca and she reached out for Anna's hand, which was slow to meet hers.

"Hey, here comes Anna," several girls called out as they ran over and grabbed her by the hand. Anna smiled broadly on seeing her friends again after a long summer and dropped Rebecca's hand. Then she remembered her duty and called back to Rebecca, "Follow me! There's the bell."

Boys and girls of all sizes pushed through the double doors and into a hallway that was brown on the bottom and cream colored above a wooden strip that ran down the hall about half way up. The ceiling was high up, at least to a little girl. Anna stopped at the first classroom door and gave Rebecca a gentle shove, "This'n yours."

Rebecca gulped, passed through and stopped dead in her tracks until a grown-up came in behind her and said, "This is your room, Betty Jean," to her daughter, whom she was leading by the hand. Rebecca watched the mother lead her child over to a desk, kiss her good-bye and go out the door. Rebecca followed and took a desk that was behind Betty Jean.

The teacher stood up in the front and rapped a long pointer on her desk.

"Good morning, boys and girls. I am your teacher, Miss Holter."

They passed out pieces of paper with blue lines and fat pencils and began to learn to write their names. This was hard for Rebecca because she had held a pencil in her hand to make marks on paper only a few times in her life. The fat pencil did not seem to want to do what she was trying to make it do.

Around the top of the blackboard on the front, side and back walls of the room, marched what teacher called the alphabet. Miss Holter told Rebecca, "Your name begins with the letter R," and Miss Holter pointed R out with the long pointer, which she occasionally tapped on the head of some noisy boys sitting together in the back of the room.

The straight line was pretty easy but it took all morning for Rebecca to capture the round top and walking leg, as Rebecca thought of the other parts of the letter R. At recess, she only had two Rs on her paper and she was relieved to go outside and get away from the strain.

There was a fat, round, red ball and the first graders made a circle on the part of the playground closest to the building. They rolled the ball back and forth to each other for a while. Then teacher said they could do what they wanted and most of the boys whooped and the girls broke off in little bunches.

Betty Jean, who was wearing a big bow in her curls and new shoes and dress, seemed from that very first morning to be admired by the other children. To be offered her hand in friendship moved one up from the base line that most of the rest of the class seemed to occupy. Betty Jean, without seeming to try, gathered a small bunch of girls who moved over to the fence and talked. They looked at the other children as they talked, giggled, and made Rebecca feel uncomfortable. But Rebecca forgot about them when she heard someone say, "Wanna' play with me?"

Rebecca turned to see a friendly smile on the face of a girl who sat two rows over and slightly behind her. Rebecca hadn't had much time to look around after the serious writing started, but she had noticed Elaine because she looked nice.

"What did you bring for lunch?" Elaine asked her as they sat down in the shade.

Rebecca turned to her and said, "I don't know."

They exchanged names. Elaine had a telephone but Rebecca didn't and had no idea how to make a call. They told each other a little about their homes and families.

Rebecca said "I have a big sister and a little brother," and didn't mention about Momma. Then teacher came out and blew a whistle and recess was over.

They went in and sang. At first, teacher had them climb steps with their voices, la, la, la, la. "Louder, boys and girls, big voices." Some of the children were shy and some were embarrassed, but the singing made Rebecca happy. They learned "Grandma's Garden." Teacher would sing the words first and the children sang line by line.

"My Ma was once a little girl..."

It was so wonderful that Rebecca tried to sing the songs for Bobby when she got home, but the tunes and words had escaped and it was a couple of weeks before she could make them come when she wanted them.

CHAPTER SEVEN
LIFE GOES ON

Rebecca did well in school. She played school with Bobby at home when they weren't helping Geneva or Poppa. Bobby learned to write his name before school started, thanks to Rebecca, and she loved teaching him.

Because she was gone in the day, Bobby began to spend more time up at the big house with Grandma and the aunties.

Once, Rebecca went home after school with Elaine to visit her house. Elaine's mother fixed them "an after-school snack" she called it, and asked them about their day. "How was school?"

Elaine answered her mother shortly that it was fine, but Rebecca, who didn't usually have an adult listener, talked on about their activities. "Betty Jean had a new dress that was blue with flowers. Teacher read some Eugene Field poems to us. We didn't get to sing today. My hand got so tared from writin'. Poppa gave me money to buy a frozen fruit cup for dessert at lunch today. That's my favorite in all the world."

Elaine's mother seemed amused and smiled a tiny smile at Rebecca's words. The girls played outside, yelling into the rain barrel. Rebecca suggested they play school and Elaine's dolls were lined up in the bedroom, learning, when Poppa came to pick up Rebecca. It was wonderful. Rebecca wished she could stay for a whole week.

CHAPTER EIGHT
GENEVA HAS A BEAU

Rebecca and Bobby didn't particularly know why Glen came around at first, but after a while, they noticed that he talked mostly to Geneva. After his first few visits, Glen and Geneva would take a walk together.

Rebecca asked, "Can Bobby and me walk with you?"

But Poppa said, "You need to come with me up the hill to Grandma's."

When they had some time together at recess, Rebecca told Elaine about her sister's beau, Glen. This was a new idea and it needed checking with a friend.

"Do you think he'll ask her to get married?" Elaine asked.

Rebecca had never been to a wedding, but she had seen some pictures of weddings. They were lovely. She heard Elaine add, "You'd be so lucky if you got to be in a wedding." Elaine wished that she had a big sister.

They decided to look in the Sears catalogue the next time they played together and see if the catalogue had wedding dresses. Then they would make paper dolls to wear them.

But they never remembered, because one day Geneva went off with Glen somewhere and they got married without anyone else around. Geneva didn't even have a white dress. She just wore her Sunday clothes.

That evening at supper, which was leftovers served by Poppa, he said to Rebecca and Bobby, "Your sister got married today so she'll be moving out."

This was an unpleasant surprise to the children. "Why can't they just stay here?" Rebecca asked.

"Geneva's a married lady now," was all the answer her father would give.

This made a big difference to the little household. Poppa wasn't much of a cook and he'd never done laundry. A little dirt didn't much bother the three of them, but the house felt empty. The children really missed Momma all over again.

CHAPTER NINE
REBECCA TRIES

"Git back," Rebecca yelled at Bobby, as she struggled across the floor with the heavy pot.

He wasn't used to his playmate talking to him like a big sister, but Rebecca knew that a big sister was needed and she was trying to be one.

So far it wasn't working out too well. Rebecca had burned food, or not gotten it completely cooked, or made something that tasted fairly nasty every time she had tried so far. So Poppa asked her to just wait for him to cook when he got home and the children often got hungry before he arrived.

Today she was going to try her hand at laundry. She couldn't begin to lift the big kettle that Momma and Geneva had used for washing, so she was trying out the biggest cooking pot. She had heated up the water and was going to carry it outside so that it wouldn't matter how much she splashed. She plopped it down not too far from the back door.

"This pot is way heavy when it's got water," she stated to her little brother. "Come on back in and help me carry out the clothes and soap."

It took them two trips, although the family hadn't many clothes. Poppa's overalls, however, were heavy.

"Now then, you drop in the clothes while I shave the soap," she directed her little brother. They both forgot the rule about washing the light clothes first.

Bobby dropped in the overalls and the water got really dark. Rebecca put in the soap and stirred the whole soup with a big stick. The water slopped over and pretty soon the front of her dress was damp.

"It's chilly today, 'specially when you git wet," Rebecca noticed.

After she fished out the overalls, she dropped in her school dress, thinking how proud Poppa would be to see that the wash was done. When she lifted the dress out, she noticed the background was no longer yellow but sort of green and not a very nice green either.

Just then Poppa came home. "What are you two up to?" he asked. "Oh, oh, didn't you forgit somethin'?"

Looking a little guilty, Rebecca asked, "What did I forgit, Poppa?"

"I think you forgot that the overalls would make the water turn blue."

Rebecca broke into tears, feeling like there was so much to remember and she wished that she had paid more attention to what Geneva, and Momma before her, had done.

CHAPTER TEN
RHEUMATIC FEVER

Rebecca's legs felt heavy as she tried to climb the stairs to bed. When she finally flopped down, those heavy legs twisted around each other and Rebecca fell asleep where Poppa found her when he got home.

She knew he was there because she felt his hand on her forehead and the next thing she was aware of was the doctor coming into the room. His big black eyes scared her.

"We're going to have to straighten these legs out or they'll stay stiff like this, even when she gets well."

Poppa got on one side and the doctor on the other and each of them took a leg and pulled them out of their tight embrace. They told her later that she screamed so loud that she could be heard for quite a distance on all sides of the house.

Bobby went to Geneva's and Poppa was spelled by various aunties while Rebecca was so sick. It seemed like a long time before they carried her out into the sunshine to sit in a chair.

Rebecca figured later that this was probably when Bobby decided to leave her and Poppa, and go to Geneva and Glen's to live.

They brought him home after she was well enough that he couldn't catch her germs anymore, but when

Poppa came home that evening, he asked, "Where's Bobby?"

And Rebecca told him that Bobby had set off walking to go back to Geneva's and Poppa didn't make him come home.

CHAPTER ELEVEN
WHY?

At home it was lonely with Bobby gone, but not at school. School was still wonderful. Rebecca knew for sure that she wanted to be a teacher when she grew up. The teacher and students got to sing a couple of times every week, and Fridays were special because of the frozen fruit salad served in the lunchroom. Rebecca was doing well in reading and writing; it hadn't taken her long to make up for her absence while she was ill. She and Elaine and sometimes other children had a good time at recess. But school ended for the summer in May.

Time hung heavy until Poppa said that she might get to stay with her cousin in town for a while. Dot, Rebecca's cousin, was little, but fun to play with and, in the town, they could get ice cream and other interesting things.

One night, just after she had fallen asleep, she was awakened by voices downstairs. Struggling to recognize the voices, she rolled out onto her bare feet and drifted down the steps. It was cousin Dot and her parents, Uncle Leon and Aunt Eva.

"Hey, sleepy head, rise and shine, we've come to get you for a visit!" Uncle Leon boomed out.

Rebecca turned on the steps and retraced her path. Upstairs she shook open a large paper bag and opened the drawer with her few summer clothes. She dumped them into the bag, pulled her nightie up over her head and dropped it in, too. Standing in her underdrawers, she chose one of the two pinafores from the bag and slipped it over her head. Shoes and socks onto the feet and she was ready.

This time her trip down the stairs was bouncy and quick.

Poppa reach for the bag to check. "Where's your winter woolens?" he asked her, as he looked up from the bag.

As what he was saying began to sink in, Rebecca's heart fell. This, then, was to be no short visit.

After Poppa added her woolens to the bag, Rebecca hugged him and gave him a kiss. She wanted to hold on, but only babies did that.

Dot's parents had a car. Normally she would be excited at the thought of a car ride, but as she, Dot, and her aunt and uncle climbed into their auto, Rebecca couldn't think about anything but why was Poppa sending her away?

When they got to the house and the sleepy girls had made their way to bed, Rebecca wasn't too tired to turn her face to the wall and let the tears flow, but no one would ever know.

CHAPTER TWELVE
IN TOWN

"Push me higher, Becky," Dot demanded of her cousin, usually more than once a day. Rebecca reminded herself that she was nine-years-old, older than Dot, and needed to act more grown up. If Rebecca didn't remind herself, certainly someone else would. So she mostly did what Dot wanted and let the littler girl take the first turn or the longest ride on the swing. She told herself it was good practice for being a teacher someday and better than being lonesome at home, but it wasn't home, that was the important thing.

"Come in, girls. Dinner's ready," Aunt Eva called. "Both of you wash your hands and Rebecca, please set the table." Rebecca thought about how Poppa hadn't cared if the forks were on the left, the sharp side of the knife blade in toward the plate. Aunt Eva had straightened out Rebecca's table-setting skills in pretty short order, but she had done it kindly.

Rebecca shoveled her food in, but Dot had to be coaxed to try a bite of this, to eat a little more of that.

Aunt Eva announced, "We'll be goin' up to visit my parents on the farm next weekend."

Rebecca looked forward to it.

CHAPTER THIRTEEN
BACK TO A FARM

The Vandenbergs' stone house sat against a bank on the north side. There were two rooms downstairs and two up, with a loft. A summer kitchen was for cooking when the weather was hot, with a big bedroom beside it for cool sleeping. This place felt good to Rebecca the minute they arrived.

"Well, who do we have here?" Mrs. Vandenberg asked of Aunt Eva, her daughter, from where Mrs V. sat in her rocking chair. Mrs. V. was stout now, no longer spry, and it was difficult for her to get up.

Aunt Eva pushed Rebecca forward, "This is Rebecca, Edgar and Edna's daughter; she's come into town to stay with us for a while."

"Hello, Rebecca, welcome to our farm."

When Rebecca smiled shyly but didn't speak, Mrs. V. remarked to her daughter. "I believe the cat's got her tongue."

When the grownups went to their own conversation, Rebecca and Dot made a getaway to check outside.

"Dot, where's the chicken house?" Rebecca asked her cousin. There were several outdoor sheds, as there were on any farm.

"Come on, Rebecca, Grandpa said there's kittens. I know where they are."

The girls oohed and aahed when they found the nest with four little black and white bodies. One baby mewed when Dot picked him up.

"Don't make him cry, Dot. Put him back with his brother and sisters. He's scared," Rebecca urged, but Dot ignored her and squeezed the kitten to her chin.

Rebecca softly patted the other three in their nest, not wishing to frighten them.

The girls rushed around. Dot introduced Rebecca to the chickens, the smokehouse where meat was cured for the winter, and the spring house where pottery crocks sat in the cold water and kept food cool. There was no electricity out here and no refrigerator like the one at Dot's house in the town, but that certainly didn't seem remarkable to Rebecca. It was just like at home.

While they were still in the spring house, Aunt Eva called from the door of the summer kitchen, "You girls bring up a pitcher of milk for dinner."

And they did. Rebecca carried it carefully, not wanting to spill any.

The breeze blew into the summer kitchen from the windows on both sides. The table was covered with a nice cloth and the girls put the plates, glasses and silverware around for six people. Rebecca was glad now that she knew the right way to set the table. It would have been embarrassing if she was still the ignorant little girl who came into town a short while back.

Uncle Leon talked about his job at the stove factory to Mr. V. The women finally sat down when everything was on the table, after the men had begun. The children listened unless spoken to because they knew that *children were to be seen and not heard.*

On the way back to town that evening, as the girls sat in the back seat with their heads heavy on their shoulders, Aunt Eva turned back and said to Rebecca, "How would you like to stay on the farm and do for my parents?"

From this dreamy place close to sleep, it sounded pretty good to Rebecca.

CHAPTER FOURTEEN
ANOTHER MOVE

So it was decided that, on the next trip up to the farm, Rebecca was to stay behind. She was young and spry and could fetch water and wood, could slop the hogs with dinner leftovers, could be an extra pair of legs that was badly needed. Once upon a time Mrs. V. could do all of these things herself, but now that she was older and heavier, it was hard and she became winded so easily.

Dot said, "I want Rebecca to stay with me in town." It was fun having a sister and a playmate.

Rebecca felt that she could be extra generous with Dot, now that she knew it was to be only a short while until she was back on a farm.

Three weeks later, they piled into the car again. Rebecca was carrying her bag and had added a book to her few possessions. Aunt Eva had said, "Now, Dot, you have several books, you can surely find one to share with Rebecca."

It was a book of Eugene Field poems, with a big giant on the cover. He was leaning on his hand. Rebecca loved to read the poems, but didn't have much opportunity because Dot wanted her attention almost all of the time. Occasionally Rebecca read to Dot from the several books on her cousin's shelf.

When they arrived at the farm after the trip up and down Maryland hills, they had fried chicken for dinner and Rebecca served with the women this time because she felt a little more grown-up. After dinner, Rebecca washed the dishes, while Dot kept her company. Rebecca thought to herself with a chuckle how much better she was at keeping house now than she had been right after Geneva left home.

Rebecca only felt a tiny pang when Aunt Eva, Uncle Leon and Dot drove off, as Rebecca and Mr. and Mrs. V. stood in the yard and waved.

"Rebecca, would you run down and shut the shed door?" Mrs. V. asked her, "Then I'll get you set up for bed."

Rebecca was to have her own spot in the loft by a window. Her cot was narrow, but covered by a pink and white quilt with sunbonnet babies. There were pegs on the wall and a small three drawer chest. There was no lamp, but they would go to bed at dark so none was needed. Rebecca carefully took her clothes from the bag and put them in the drawers. In the bottom drawer, she placed the folded bag. After all, she might need it later.

When she had her nightie on and had said her prayers, Mrs. V. called up to say goodnight. "I hope you'll be happy here, Rebecca. It's nice to have a young-ster around again."

CHAPTER FIFTEEN
COWS DON'T WAIT

The birds began to sing and Rebecca opened her eyes. The sun had barely begun to light the world, but Rebecca knew she was going to learn to milk a cow this morning. "Cows don't wait for the sun," she told herself, as she rolled out and pulled her nightie over her head.

She choose one of the two everyday dresses from the drawer, slipped it over her head and reached up to button it at the back of her neck. Folding her nightie carefully, she placed it under the pillow and drew up the quilt. She smoothed the bed and stood back to see if it looked neat. She slipped her stocking feet into shoes and headed down from the loft.

Mr. Vandenberg was waiting in the kitchen with a pail and a mug of coffee. He didn't say anything as they went out the back door and down to the barn for the lesson.

Rebecca had seen other people milking before; plenty of people had cows. She didn't expect it to be hard.

"No, no, you have to strip the teat like this," Mr. V. said, as he reached over her shoulder and showed her again.

Rebecca felt terribly discouraged when the cow began to get impatient and Mr. V. took back over from her and finished the milking.

Later, at the breakfast table, Mrs. V. said, "There's just a little trick to milking. It'll come. After we get the dishes washed up, we'll start the washin'." It was Monday.

"Keep the shavings over the tub, Rebecca," Mrs. V. scolded Rebecca as she shaved strips of soap off the bar of Fels Naptha and into the hot water. "I'll show you how to make soap this fall. I never used to buy it."

Rebecca rubbed the clothes up and down on the washboard and had most of the laundry hung out when they went into the kitchen to put dinner on. While they were fixing dinner, Rebecca shared with Mrs. V her dream of becoming a teacher.

"That's nice. We better hurry, Mr. V. will come in hungry as a bear pretty shortly," Mrs. V. said as she sat down to peel potatoes. "Rebecca, go fill that pail up."

Rebecca watched a sparrow hopping not too far away, as she went along to the spring under the spring house to fetch the water and carry it up to the house. The day was hot and Rebecca took the opportunity to wet her hands and face.

When the dishes were done and put away, Mrs. V. said Rebecca could go up and rest. Mrs. V. herself liked to take it easy for a while after dinner. Rebecca was glad because now she would have some time to read her book. She lay across the bed and held the book up. A fly buzzed around, tickling her from time to time, and sang her a lullaby. The book became heavy to hold up and Rebecca thought she would just rest her eyes. It must have been almost an hour later when she heard herself being called from below by Mrs. V.

"Rebecca, Rebecca, come on down."

CHAPTER SIXTEEN
SATURDAY NIGHT AND SUNDAY AFTERNOON

It was Saturday night and Rebecca was heating water in the big teakettle for her bath when she heard, "My stars! The wild men are coming."

Rebecca knew Mrs. V. was talking about her own grandsons. She had heard about Arthur and Carrie's six boys. Actually the smallest was still a baby so he hadn't gotten into much yet, but he would probably end up just like the others. They would go through gates without shutting them and run hog wild over the farm, wreaking havoc. Arthur and Carrie had sent word that they would be coming up the next day.

Secretly she was glad. It meant that tomorrow she would have other children to play with, even if they were wild.

When the kettle began to sing, Rebecca picked up a dish towel and lifted it off the stove. It was a heavy load to carry, but at least the spring house was down hill.

The long spring house was built of logs to protect that part of the stream that provided the house with water and kept the food cold, but it was also the place to take a bath. Rebecca opened the squeaky door and crossed over to the big wash tub. She had already carried down her nightie and a towel. She emptied the kettle of hot water into the tub and added a couple of buckets of cool water from the stream. She stripped off her clothes and gingerly stepped in. Maybe this was the best part of the week, Rebecca thought to herself as she relaxed a moment and sat back. She scrubbed herself thoroughly and rinsed off, hopped out and dried hard with the rough towel. Even though it had been a hot summer day, the evenings were beginning to feel a bit chilly, especially if you were wet.

Rebecca slipped her feet into her shoes and pulled her nightgown over her head. She filled the bucket a couple of times with the bath water, which she carried out and poured on the kitchen garden. Finally the tub was empty enough for her to just lift and carry it out. She emptied it right outside the spring house, rinsed it with a little water from a pail and replaced everything back inside. She gathered her dirty clothes and the towel and started back up to the summer kitchen. She hung the towel on a peg inside the door.

"Goodnight, Mr. and Mrs. V," she called out to the other room as she climbed up to the loft. Rebecca sat for a moment and looked out of the window at the stars just beginning to show. "I wonder what Poppa's doin'," she thought to herself. She seldom thought about Momma anymore except for occasionally wondering if her own mother would have been grumpy like Mrs. V was sometimes. But the thoughts didn't stop her from sleeping well at night.

Rebecca sat up quickly in the morning with the exciting thought that today she would be able to play with children. She dressed quickly and was down lighting the stove before she knew it. She grabbed the milk bucket, ladled a little water in, rinsed the water around by circling the bucket and emptied the water into the cat's bowl outside of the door.

The cow was waiting impatiently as Rebecca unlatched the barn door. By now Rebecca was a skilled milker. It was a new enough skill that she still felt a little proud. She pulled the three-legged stool up to the cow and rested her head against the cow's side as she filled the bucket. When she was finished, she carried the bucket to the spring house where she put some cream in the churn.

Up and down, around and around, she worked the paddle until the butter began to form. Rebecca packed the butter into a tub and set it in the cold water and started for the chicken house.

"Good morning, Miss Henny Penny and sisters," Rebecca greeted the chickens. Although the rooster now recognized her, from time to time he took it upon himself to protect his bevy of ladies, and then he would start for Rebecca's leg. But she was ready for him this time. She kept something between herself and the rooster. She filled the small trough with chicken feed and scattered some grain around the chickens' yard.

Then it was breakfast time. She could smell the biscuits as she approached the back door. Rebecca took her seat at the table where the Vandenbergs had just begun to fill their plates.

Not only did the wild men come, but Dot also came with her parents.

The children ran throughout the day, except for when they came in to dinner. They followed Rebecca to the spring house and each carried up something to help her: the pitcher of milk, the butter, some cool water, the deviled eggs.

After dinner Mrs. V. said, "We'll do the dishes,

Rebecca; you should go on and play.

"Tag, you're it!" one of the boys said as he swatted Dot's arm. Toward sundown the girls decided they had had enough running. The wild men didn't even listen when Rebecca suggested playing school. She and Dot were sitting on the fence together, singing "Red Sails in the Sunset," when the parents gathered the grandchildren up to leave.

Rebecca was so tired that she could hardly climb to the loft to go to bed.

CHAPTER SEVENTEEN
TEN CENTS A BUSHEL

Rebecca was lying on her stomach and turning the pages of the Sears catalogue, looking at school dresses when she said to Mrs. V., "I really like the plaid dress with the white collar."

"Well, Rebecca, you know you can pick beans here in the neighborhood and earn some money. I know the folks down the road have been looking for help."

So the very next day, when her chores were finished, Rebecca headed down the hill to the farm with waiting green beans.

"Ten cents a bushel," the neighbor lady told Rebecca. "Start at the far end of the row."

Rebecca lugged the bushel basket to the far end and began to pick. The bean vines made her arms itch, but at least the pole beans didn't make her bend over so that she ended up with a back ache like she had when she picked beans at the Vandenbergs.

There were other young people picking, too, and Rebecca listened and laughed and enjoyed being part of the group, even if most of the others were a little older than her.

One particular girl kept smiling at Rebecca when they were working close to each other. She said her name was Florence and that she was thirteen.

"On Sunday, after church, do you want to take a walk in the woods with me?" Florence asked.

"Yes, I'd really like to." Rebecca had enjoyed walking in the woods by herself over the summer, but being with another girl would really be special.

"I'll come over to the Vandenbergs at about two after dinner is cleaned up and we'll have ourselves a good time. Have you been up over that hill yonder with all the rocks?"

"No, what's up there?"

"I don't know, but let's go." So it was all set.

At the end of the afternoon Rebecca was tired, but pleased. She had picked three bushels and would be back again. She was determined to earn as much as she could in the few weeks before school began. She wanted that plaid dress with the white collar very much. "Wouldn't I look great starting back to school in that dress?" Rebecca thought to herself. It was the first time she remembered thinking so much about what she was going to wear. "Maybe pretty soon I'll be a young lady."

CHAPTER EIGHTEEN
AN ADVENTURE

There was a soft knocking at the summer kitchen door and Florence called out, "Rebecca."

Rebecca looked over at Mrs. V. They weren't quite finished with washing and drying the dishes.

"Go on, child, I can finish up here."

That was all it took. Rebecca hung her dish towel and was out the back door. "Hi," she said shyly to Florence and smiled her biggest smile.

The day was almost perfect, a little hot, but it would be cooler in the woods. The two girls walked across a field toward their goal: the hill with rocks and a stand of trees.

"I'm really glad you could come with me, Rebecca. Please don't think I'm nosy but how come you live up here with the Vandenbergs?"

"Well, I do for them because they're getting on and can't do everything for themselves. Anyway it's harder for them now. I used to live on the other side of the mountain with my Poppa. My Momma died when I was little. When I grow up I want to be a teacher." It was probably the longest speech Rebecca had given, but she felt like she trusted Florence.

Florence pointed to the berry patch at the edge of the field, "There's where we picked berries right after the fourth of July. Let's go in that direction."

Almost as soon as they were in the trees, the air felt cooler and, without the sun beating down on them, they slowed their walk. There was an old rail fence near the edge of the trees. Two crossed posts stuck almost upright, supporting zig-zagged, laid down rails. The girls had just started to climb over the fence when Rebecca looked down at what looked like another rail sitting on top of the bottom rail of the fence. The rail moved.

"Ohhh! It's a snake," Rebecca called back over her shoulder to Florence who began immediately to search for a branch long enough to deal with a snake.

Florence came up with a long, sturdy limb which the two girls grabbed together and used to push the snake off the bottom rail. They could feel how heavy the creature was as they stuck the stick under the snake and raised it.

"Oh, Rebecca! Look, he's almost as big around as our arms."

The snake finally tumbled off the fence, and when he hit the ground, he looked at them and began to hum and then rattle.

"A rattlesnake!" they both said with proper alarm.

Rebecca forgot to breathe and was stuck to a spot on the ground, even though she knew that old rattler could really move if he wanted to.

Luckily for them, the rattler was in no mood to fight and moved lazily off in the other direction.

Still Florence and Rebecca waited a while before climbing over the fence and continuing their walk. And, from there on, they kept their eyes wide open.

When they arrived back at the Vandenbergs, words tumbled out of each of them as they told the story, more details remembered with every telling.

The Vandenbergs listened closely and Mrs. V. exclaimed "Good lands sake!"

"Heard say, one of those fellers bites you, it's like boilin' water in yer veins. Only it's not water. I'd better ask one of the neighbors to take care of that one," Mr. V. said knowingly to his wife.

CHAPTER NINETEEN
A NEW DRESS, A NEW SCHOOL

Rebecca and Mrs. V. were in the kitchen canning tomatoes one morning when Mrs. V. noticed that Rebecca hadn't smiled or said much all morning. "Why so glum, Rebecca?" she asked.

"I've worked and worked really hard, but I haven't got enough money for the plaid dress," Rebecca answered. "I'm still short some."

"You know, I have a little extra set aside from my egg money, Rebecca, I believe I can help you out. When we finish with this job, you run up and get your money and we'll see what we can do."

Rebecca washed, peeled and quartered the remaining tomatoes happily. Starting school with a new dress would make a big difference, she was sure.

The last jar was sealed and the kitchen table wiped up. As she disappeared around the corner, Rebecca said, "I'll get my money and be right down,"

Up in her room, she took the Mason jar off the small chest and shook the coins out on the quilt. "Twenty-five, fifty, a dollar, five, ten, a dollar ten..." The coins made a heavy load in her hands as she came down from the loft and placed them on the table.

Mrs. V. sat with her pocketbook beside her as she crocheted on a square for an afghan she was making.

"Now go get the catalogue," Mrs. V. told Rebecca.

Rebecca could turn to the exact page already. She knew it was page 374.

"All right, now we need to figure this out. The dress costs $2.15 and we have to pay a quarter for them to send it, so that's $2.40. How much do you have saved up?"

"I have $1.80," Rebecca answered proudly. It had been hard work to save up that much money. It was the most that she had ever had at one time in her life.

"So how much more do you need?"

Rebecca was smart and she answered immediately, "Sixty cents."

"Well, I believe I can fix you up. I just sold two dozen eggs," Mrs. V said, as she handed Rebecca two quarters and a dime.

When the order form was filled out, the money carefully folded into a paper, and the envelope sealed, Rebecca headed out to the road to put it in the mailbox and turn up the flag.

Two and a half weeks passed slowly; Rebecca walked out to the mailbox on the road every day, watching for the package. The dress finally arrived. Rebecca carried the package in excitedly and tried it on. It was perfect, after Mrs. V helped her pin up the hem and shorten it a little.

"It's good, Rebecca, that the dress is just a little too big because you'll get some good out of it next year, too, that is, if you don't go growing up too much!"

The night before school began, Rebecca laid the dress out all ready for the morning. She was going to have to milk the cow and feed the chickens first and then come back in and put on the new dress, so she would have to get up a little earlier than usual. She said her prayers and climbed into bed, but she felt excited and it was hard to get to sleep.

That night she dreamed that she was grown up. She was the teacher in front of a classroom and held the Eugene Field poems in her hand and read to the class, "Father calls me William, Mother calls me Will, Sister calls me Willie but the fellers call me Bill."

She awoke a little later than usual instead of a little earlier. "Oh no!" Rebecca exclaimed to herself as she pulled her old work dress over her head and slipped her feet into the shoes. She hurried down from the loft, grabbed the pail on the way out of the door.

Rebecca had never hurried so fast through the milking. She barely had time to greet the hens as she sprinkled their feed. When she came in the door, Mrs. V. called out that breakfast was ready.

"I don't have time to eat, Mrs. V. I have to change my dress. May I take a biscuit and jelly for dinner?" Rebecca called over her shoulder as she scrambled back to the loft.

She came down again in the new dress, splashed her

face and dried it on the towel, grabbed her food and called out, "Good-bye" as she went out the door. Rebecca ran across the field as fast as she could, a pain was beginning in her side so that she had to slow down once she hit the road. She knew it was a couple of miles and there wasn't any way she could run all of it. Normally Rebecca liked to walk this road through the woods, but there was no time to notice anything this morning.

Before she finally got to it, she could see the crossing with a bigger road where the school bus would stop. Several children of various ages and sizes were already waiting, including Florence. Then Rebecca saw the bus pull up while she was still a distance away.

"Hold the bus," she called as loudly as she could, while she began to run again, trying to ignore the pain in her side that came whenever she picked up her speed.

"Hold the bus," she called again in case they hadn't heard her the first time, but this time she couldn't even yell because she was even more breathless.

It took the youngsters a little time to file on, but Rebecca still wasn't quite there when the last one, a little girl with pigtails, disappeared up the steps. Rebecca didn't stop though, just in case she still might make it. And she did.

She was gasping as she climbed on and heard Florence say to her, "I told the bus driver that you were coming as fast as you could and to please wait."

The bus driver, a man with a plaid shirt, a cap and glasses, turned to Rebecca and said, "Young lady, I can't wait every mornin', you'd better leave earlier."

Rebecca barely nodded as she sat down beside Florence and tried to catch her breath.

CHAPTER TWENTY
TRYING

Rebecca welcomed the walk back from the bus after school, down the road and through the woods. She needed time to talk silently to herself about the new school.

"I used to think I was smart...I don't know what to think now." The other students had known more than she did. How could she be a teacher if other people knew more than she did? Some of the other students even studied foreign languages. Rebecca loved to read, but there hadn't been many books around at home or now, here on the mountain. The Vandenbergs did have an encyclopedia and Rebecca took volumes off the shelf when she had time. She loved to look at the pictures and read about people in far off lands. She was fascinated by the lady driving a tractor in Russia. The words under the picture said that the Russians were our friends.

"How am I going to catch up with those other kids? I don't want them to think I'm a dummy."

When Rebecca came in the back door she didn't need Mrs. V's reminder to take off her good school dress before going out to do chores. She knew there wouldn't be another new dress any time soon.

"Yes, I know," she said to Mrs. V., who was snapping peas.

"Are we a little grumpy?"

"No, ma'am. Sorry, I was thinking. I'll be right down to help soon's I change."

After supper and the dishes, Rebecca sat with her books and homework at the kitchen table but she couldn't work long because the days were getting shorter and daylight was running out. Mr. V didn't like for them to use the kerosene lamps until winter. Kerosene cost money and besides he'd say, "The lamps are a mess to clean." But it was going to be hard to catch up with the other students without plenty of time to study.

Most nights in the summer the three had sat outside, listening to the whippoorwills until bedtime at dark, and never missed having inside lights.

Rebecca woke up earlier for her second day of school and managed to get her chores done in time to eat breakfast. She knew that she still had to move as fast as she could to get to the bus stop. She was the last one up the steps again, but the driver hadn't had to wait this time.

The problem today was math class. Everyone else seemed to know about long division but it looked like a secret code to Rebecca, a secret code that she wasn't ever going to crack.

"Young lady," the teacher, Mr. McCurdy, said, "you have to study. It won't just pop into your head!" He was a little man with glasses. He looked out at the class over the top of his glasses and Rebecca tried not to dislike him, but it was hard when he frowned directly at her.

CHAPTER TWENTY-ONE
TOO HARD

It was the earliest freeze folks could remember for quite a while. September 25. And it didn't make things easier for Rebecca.

Of course she didn't want to get out from under her warm quilt in the early morning, but she did anyway. The bus driver had made it very clear after the last time he had to wait, when he said, "I'm never, ever going to wait again. Period."

But, even when she got up plenty early, before the rooster and other birds, getting the chores done was harder in the cold. As fall made its way toward winter, water and milk in the spring house froze. Rebecca had to break the surface of the spring before she could draw water for use in the house. Saturday night baths were in the kitchen now.

"I believe I'm going to knit you a pair of mittens, 'Becca," Mrs. V. said, and it was welcome news for the girl.

It was the morning that Rebecca slipped on the ice in the road during her final run for the bus and fell, knocking the wind right out of her, that she looked up to see the bus pull away without her. She simply couldn't get right back up. Tears began to form in her eyes and spill over her checks. Rebecca put her face down in the new mittens and let the tears come.

It was too hard, just too hard, to do her jobs and go to school. Anyway, what good was school? She didn't need it. "I'm not going back," she said firmly to herself and the squirrel, who seemed to be sitting back on his tail and watching her as she sat in the road. "Do you hear me, Chatter?" she asked as he regarded her with his beady eyes. Rebecca decided that she preferred the company of squirrels to teachers whose eyes looked sternly at her over their glasses.

CHAPTER TWENTY-TWO
LEARN TO FLY

At first it was a relief to leisurely wake up with the rooster's call, dress, climb down and go through her chores without feeling as if something terrible was going to happen if she didn't go faster, faster.

There was plenty to keep her busy: Monday's wash, Tuesday's ironing, Wednesday's scrubbing floors or windows, right through the week.

"Rebecca, I wish you'd think about this. Someday you might be sorry about quitting school so young. You can't be a teacher without first going to school." Mrs. V. said to her several times the first week, a couple of times the second week and once during the third.

Rebecca tried to close her ears without holding her hands over them. She couldn't think about that. Somewhere was a big black cloud waiting to smother her if she thought about that and she would not let that cloud anywhere near her. No!

It was lonely, though, when all of the work was done. She closed the back door as she went out and across the field to walk in the woods. The stubble crunched under her feet and the sun shone weakly. She hadn't gotten too far into the woods when she stopped short at the sight of a tree full of Cedar Waxwings. They came to spend the winter sometimes, but she had never seen such a lovely sight. She stood silently and watched for a long time and they fed, flitted and trilled, unaware of her. And then, as if by signal, the whole flock rose and flew away.

Rebecca's heart sunk as the birds rose. She knew her wings were clipped. She couldn't ever fly and she had done it herself. She walked back toward the farm with tears in her eyes and hoped no one would be in the kitchen, but when she opened the door, Florence was there! At the sight of Florence, Rebecca realized how lonely she had been. Mrs. V. was sitting in her rocker, smiling at the two girls.

"Hi," was all Rebecca could say.

"Rebecca, everyone asked me about you. Please come back to school. Why did you stop?" The words tumbled out of Florence's mouth, as she got up from the cookies and milk Mrs. V. had laid out on the table.

"Why don't you girls sit down and have a visit? I'm going in the other room for a bit," Mrs. V. said as she rose heavily from the rocker, gathering her yarn and needles in one hand.

She had barely made it to the door when Rebecca answered Florence. "I'm so glad to see you. I've missed you. I've been lonely, but I can't go to school. I just can't get everything done in the mornings. I tried, but it's too much. I run and I'm still late for the bus and the bus driver is angry. I just can't do it!"

Mrs. V. stopped in her tracks and turned back. "My goodness, Rebecca, why didn't you tell me? We can do something about it, I'm sure."

She didn't mean to, but Rebecca burst into tears and burried her face in her arms. It didn't seem possible that things could work out.

Florence reached across the table and patted Rebecca's arm. "I'm older. I can help you catch up. We can start right now."

"Rebecca," Mrs. V. said, "Mr. V. and I are not so old that we can't do the milking on school mornings. It's important for you to go to school."

Rebecca heard them both and it began to sink in. She could go back to school. She didn't have to be lonely. Life could be exciting. Rebecca raised her head and smiled at Florence and Mrs. V.

"I'll try," she said.

EPILOGUE

Rebecca was in her seventies when we sat down at her kitchen table, after the noonday dinner dishes were done, and she shared her childhood with me for the first time. I wanted to know the whole story, and bit by bit over several years, she told it to me. Then I wanted to share it with the children of today.

She has never lived anywhere but western Maryland, on one side of the hill or the other, and always on a farm. Her story begins in the 1920s, a time when many people lived so modestly that we can hardly imagine their lives.

If we look at the story one way, it is very sad, but we can also think of it as a human triumph over very sad conditions. In spite of all that happened to her, Rebecca grew up to be an intelligent, positive, caring person and we can rejoice in her victory.

Raya Bodnarchuk is an artist who lives in the Town of Glen Echo, Maryland. Her work is in the National Museum of American Art; on the grounds of the bi-county WSSC Headquarters in Laurel, Maryland; and will be included in a pedestrian pathway over the Capital Beltway. Ms. Bodnarchuk is on the faculty of the Corcoran School of Art in Washington, DC.